Published by
Access Consciousness Publishing, LLC
www.accessconsciousnesspublishing.com

Printed in the United States of America
Ease, Joy and Glory

The Baby
Unicorn
Manifesto

When a baby unicorn is born into the world, the other unicorns come running, galloping and hopping from all over the globe.

And one by one, they come forward and whisper
the truth of living into the baby unicorn's
tiny pointy fluffy ears.

Those words stay with the unicorn for the rest
of its life, forever ingrained in its small
rainbow-colored soft heart.

"You are a gift," they whisper.

"The likes of which the world has never seen,"
they say.

"You are a beautiful contribution to the world
and to our lives, and we are so grateful you are here."

"Your presence makes the world shine brighter."

"You bring possibilities to this place that no one has ever seen before."

"Yes," they whisper, "sometimes it will be tough,
but don't worry Baby Unicorn, we are here for you.
We have your back. You can do no wrong in our eyes."

Those last words they often repeat, accompanied
by the firm stomping of their golden hooves:
"You can do no wrong in our eyes, Baby Unicorn.
Know that, Baby Unicorn."

And then they continue: "Your only task is to choose who you would like to be, and we will do our best to support you in every choice you make.

We will be here sharing our insights and wisdom and awareness to do everything we can to make your journey as easy and joyful as possible."

"Remember," they continue,
"above all, Baby Unicorn, you are not alone.
We are here for you.
Always.

We are grateful for your existence
every moment of every day."

"Shine, beautiful being, shine!

Welcome to the world, and to the new reality
of possibilities that you, just by coming
into this world, have helped create!"

"Now is your time," they say, and shake their
manes so that a shower of glittery stars rain down
on the baby unicorn.

The stars twinkle and tickle, and the baby unicorn laughs;
a brand new beautiful laugh, never ever
heard on this planet before.

With that sound ringing in the universe,
the baby unicorn is ready to trot
forth and be magic!

And dear reader, if you're wondering where baby unicorns can be found, let me tell you a secret:

They are right here, right now, reading these very words…

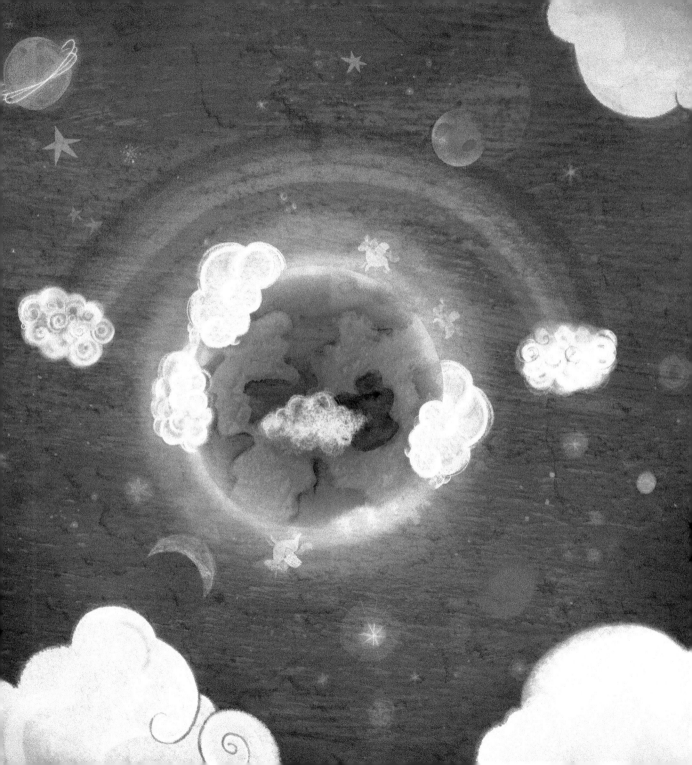

You are one.

You are a baby unicorn, my friend.

And now is your time.

AUTHORS

Dr. Dain Heer is an energetic virtuoso and world-changer with baby-whispering as a less well-known specialty. He lives in Texas, USA, and this is his first children's book.

www.drdainheer.com

Katarina Wallentin is an avid explorer of the magic that is truly possible on this beautiful planet of ours. She lives in Sweden with her daughter, who most definitely is a unicorn.

www.katarinawallentin.com

ILLUSTRATOR

Nathalie Beauvois is a freelance illustrator living in Argentina, drawing pictures for the world. She loves to illustrate for children and everything related to everyday life…especially really yummy food!

www.childrensillustrators.com

CPSIA information can be obtained
at www.ICGtesting.com
Printed in the USA
BVHW021136030119
536774BV00055B/2621/P

9 781634 931533